ANNE FINE

The Killer Cat's Christmas

Illustrated by Steve Cox

PUFFIN

Penguin Books Ltd, 80 Strand, London WC2R 0RL, England
Penguin Group (USA) Inc., 375 Hudson Street, New York, New York 10014, USA
Penguin Group (Canada), 90 Eglinton Avenue East, Suite 700, Toronto, Ontario, Canada M4P 2Y3
(a division of Pearson Penguin Canada Inc.)
Penguin Ireland, 25 St Stephen's Green, Dublin 2, Ireland (a division of Penguin Books Ltd)
Penguin Group (Australia), 250 Camberwell Road, Camberwell, Victoria 3124, Australia
(a division of Pearson Australia Group Pty Ltd)
Penguin Books India Pvt Ltd, 11 Community Centre, Panchsheel Park, New Delhi – 110 017, India
Penguin Group (NZ), 67 Apollo Drive, Rosedale, North Shore 0632, New Zealand
(a division of Pearson New Zealand Ltd)
Penguin Books (South Africa) (Pty) Ltd, 24 Sturdee Avenue, Rosebank, Johannesburg 2196, South Africa

Penguin Books Ltd, Registered Offices: 80 Strand, London WC2R 0RL, England

puffinbooks.com

First published 2009
This edition published 2010
1

Set in 15/19.7pt Baskerville by Palimpsest Book Production Limited,
Falkirk, Stirlingshire
Made and printed in England by Clays Ltd, St Ives plc

British Library Cataloguing in Publication Data
A CIP catalogue record for this book is available from the British Library

ISBN: 978-0-141-32771-6

www.greenpenguin.co.uk

Mixed Sources
Product group from well-managed
forests and other controlled sources
www.fsc.org Cert no. SA-COC-1592
© 1996 Forest Stewardship Council

Penguin Books is committed to a sustainable future
for our business, our readers and our planet.
The book in your hands is made from paper
certified by the Forest Stewardship Council.

Contents

1: Horrible, horrible, horrible!   1

2: 'Oh, goody gumdrops! Hoppers!'   6

3: 'The whole of Christmas in a cattery!'   14

4: Surprise, surprise!   19

5: Frog in a wedding dress   24

6: Screams and tears   30

7: Twanging the spider's web   35

8: Chasing half-dead mousies   45

9: Bare at the bottom   51

10: Chocolate coins and sausages   55

11: Showers of falling food   61

12: Star of the show   67

(Unlucky) 13: The fairy on the   77
     Christmas tree

1: Horrible, horrible, horrible!

OKAY, OKAY! SO run off sobbing, but I did not kill that moth on *purpose*. It was not my fault. I do agree that I reached out to biff it once or twice. But it was *annoying* me, flapping round and round my face.

And I'm not sure that it's dead anyway. I mean, I saw it sort of flapping off, looking a bit lopsided. But after that it disappeared. For all I know, the thing's still somewhere in the house, minding its own business and mucking about wherever it wants.

Unlike me, locked in this garage in disgrace, after a horrible Christmas.

So go on, ask me. 'Dear, dear Tuffy,
why was your Christmas so horrible?'

And I'll explain: because it is a festival
that wasn't made for cats. Just think
about it. There's a tree we're not allowed
to climb.

And there are tempting dangly
decorations we're not allowed to touch.

And there are glorious glittering
strands of bright, bright tinsel hung far

3

too high for us to reach. Shiny wrapped presents we have to keep our paws off.

And, if we're really unlucky, horrible cold white snow all over the garden.

No. *Not* my favourite time of year.

So go on. Ask the next question. 'But, Tuffy, what on earth *happened*? How come you've ended up locked in the garage?'

I'll tell you. It was because this Christmas was even worse than usual. This Christmas was terrible.

Frightful.

Awful.

Miserable.

All wrong.

Horrible, horrible, horrible. That's what it was.

I'll tell you the whole story.

2: 'Oh, goody gumdrops! Hoppers!'

THE CAR DREW up outside and out they all spilled, as usual. Our Christmas visitors. That's Ellie's Aunt Ann, her husband, Brian, and the soppy twins.

I hate having visitors. They park their bottoms in the comfiest chairs. They dump their suitcases in all my favourite corners. They rattle their clothes around in the cupboards I like to use to take a quiet nap. Their stupid great feet keep stumbling over my food dish.

But Ellie loves company. She couldn't wait to rush out of the house to greet her cousins. 'Lucilla! Lancelot! Oh, I'm so glad you're here!'

She might have been glad they were here. I have a forkful of brain inside my head so I wasn't quite so keen. As she ran one way, I sneaked off the other to find somewhere good to hide.

I heard them wheel their suitcases inside. 'Where's Tuffy? We must say hello to darling, darling Tuffy!'

They searched the house. But I was
stretched out flat on top of the cupboard
in the hall. They couldn't find me, so
they finally gave up.

'Forget Tuffy for a moment,' said
Lancelot. 'Let's do something else. Let's
play on the bouncy hoppers.'

'Oh, goody gumdrops! Hoppers!'

The three of them rushed off. Phew! I
jumped down from the cupboard and
went upstairs. The bathroom window
was ajar, so I crept out and spent a quiet

half hour on the garage roof, secretly watching the three of them bounce up and down the drive, clutching the sticky-up ears. It was a laugh. Ellie kept falling off. But then Lucilla started to sing some half-baked bouncing song that she'd made up about 'sweet little mousies in housies'.

It got on my nerves, so I took off. I picked my way along the tree branch and jumped down on the fence.

Lucilla saw me. 'Tuff-eee! Tuff-eee!'

She bounced towards the fence so hard she couldn't stop. Is it *my* fault the fence is wobbly? I didn't mean to stick my sharp little claws out quite so far to get a grip as I swayed this way and that.

Or keep them out when I fell off the fence, on to her hopper.

POOOOOOOOOOOOOOOOOOOOOOof . . .

Okay, okay! So pump me up with air,
and tie a knot in me. I clawed a hole in
her hopper. For heaven's sake, it was an
accident! How was it my fault that it sort
of shrivelled under her, and she fell off?

I hurried under the thorn bush.
Lucilla rolled over on to her hands and
knees and started wheedling into the
greenery. 'Oh, Tuffy, dearest! Don't you
remember us? It's me, Lucilla. Lancelot's

here too. Oh, please come out so we can cuddle you.'

'Yes,' Lancelot echoed. 'Oh, darling Tuffy. *Please* come out.'

Oh, I came out all right. But on the other side, and straight back up on the fence. From there, I jumped on the garage roof, and into the house through the bathroom window.

So go on! Boil me in bubble bath! Maybe I wasn't quite as careful as I should have been, walking along the sill. Perhaps some of the fancy bottles of shampoos and lotions did get tipped on to the floor. But it wasn't *me* who left the tops off. So how was *I* supposed to know that they were going to make a mess like that – a huge, foaming, slimy puddle of froth and goo and gel? All I was trying to do was get away to somewhere I'd be left in peace.

And maybe choosing to hide under
Ellie's mother's best silver party frock
was not the smartest idea. But *I* didn't
pull the stupid thing off its hanger. It fell
off by itself as I rushed in the closet.
Okay, so maybe I did root about a bit,
trying to make myself comfy. But how
was I to know I'd pop off all those
sequins? All I was doing was trying to
take a little *nap*. Can't a pet take a nap in

his own house without Ellie's mother ending up sitting in a heap on the carpet, picking the cat hairs off a ruined frock and sobbing her heart out?

I ask you. Honestly! How wet is *that*?

3: 'The whole of Christmas in a cattery!'

IT WOKE ME up, though, all that boo-hooing from Ellie's mum. Then Mr Grumpy rushed up the stairs to find out what was going on, and things turned nasty. There were some harsh words.

'You furry vandal!' Ellie's father snarled. 'You foul and spiteful beast!'

I played it cool, raising an eyebrow at him.

He hates it when I put on my 'not bothered' look, and flick my tail at him. 'Look what you've done!' he fumed. 'You've turned a beautiful and expensive frock into a filthy rag!' He waved it in my face. 'Look at it! Torn to shreds!'

Now Ellie had arrived, with Lucilla and Lancelot in tow. They all stuck up for me. 'Oh, please don't blame Tuffy!' begged Lancelot.

'He didn't mean to spoil the frock!' insisted Lucilla.

'He's just unsettled from having visitors,' Ellie explained to her father.

But Mr Blame-The-Cat-For-Everything was not having that. He wagged his telling-off finger. 'Don't you believe it! This whiskery little waster knows full well what he's about. And I tell you this house would be a far, far better place if we just made the sensible decision to ask the vet to simply –'

I didn't catch the last few words. Ellie had let out a fearsome screech, and clapped her hands over my ears.

15

I wriggled free in time to hear the end of his next threat: '– or spend the whole of Christmas in a cattery!'

Up came Ellie's hands again. This time, when I tugged back my head enough to hear, the only words I caught were: '– in some strong cage!'

Ellie was almost in tears. And so were Lancelot and Lucilla.

'Oh, *please* don't say that, Uncle George!'

'No, don't say that!'

But Ellie's father was still in a rage. 'Well, it's my view that –'

'No!' Ellie cried. 'We three will look after Tuffy! You needn't worry. We'll keep him well away from you.'

Her father was still scowling. 'And well away from all the clothes in the cupboards? And the tree? And all the food? And all the presents and the decorations?'

'Yes! Tuffy won't spoil *anything*, I promise!'

Ellie pounced on me. And since for once I felt I would be safer out of there, I let her scoop me up and carry me off, down to the living room, well away from Mrs Still-Red-And-Weepy-Eyes, clutching the torn shreds of her ruined frock, and Mr Total-Grump.

4: Surprise, surprise!

SO THAT'S HOW I ended up sitting like
Goody-Two-Shoes on the sofa in the
front room, while Lucilla and Lancelot
drooled and drivelled over my brains
and beauty.

'Oh, Tuffy! You're so lovely.'

'Your fur's so *soft*.'

'And you're so *clever*.'

'I wish *we* had a cat.'

'Oh, Ellie! You're so *lucky*!'

It just went on and on. I stood it for
about a minute or two, and then I
reckoned it was time to leave, so I stood
up.

Quick as a flash, all three of them
reached out to stop me. I was trapped.

'No, Tuffy! We promised!'

'Just to keep you safe!'

'You have to stay!'

I tried to wriggle free. Lucilla shut the
door and Lancelot checked the window
latch. Ellie could see that I was getting
nervous, so, 'Never mind,' she soothed.
'Let's think of something to play.'

Play? What does she think I am? Some newborn *fluff* ball? But it is always best to know what's going on, so I stopped struggling long enough to listen. What was it going to be? Hide and Seek? (I hoped not. Most of the hiding places in this house are mine, mine, *mine*.) How about Murder in the Dark? (Step on me by mistake, and I will scratch a good chunk out of you!) Perhaps they'd choose Tiddleywinks. (Better take care. Flick just one wink at me, and you are *dead*.)

Surprise, surprise!

'Let's put on a show!' Lucilla said.

'Yes!' Lancelot echoed. 'Let's put on a little show!'

Ellie was bouncing up and down, clapping her hands. 'Oh, goody gumdrops! I love doing special little shows!'

I was embarrassed. (Ellie's such a *drip*.) But I did think I might at least be left to sit up on the dresser and sneer. I mean, you can't train cats to act or dance. No one would even try. You might be able to boss dogs about. But never cats.

So I thought I'd be safe with special little shows.

Well, more fool me.

5: *Frog in a wedding dress*

SO GUESS WHAT The Three Softies finally
decided that they were going to do.

Yes. Just my luck. A show of nursery
rhymes that have a cat in them. Is that
tattered old book that you grew out of
years ago still on your shelf? Shall we
run through some of the sweet little baby
songs your granny used to warble to you
when you were still in nappies?

There's 'Ding Dong Bell, Pussy's in the
Well', of course. Then there's that merry
old favourite, 'Hey Diddle Diddle, the
Cat and the Fiddle'. After that, there is
the tragic tale of 'Three Little Kittens

who Lost their Mittens'. And 'Pussy Cat, Pussy Cat, Where Have You Been?'

Not to mention the sickly, revolting, soppy and Ellie-ish one I really, really hoped they had forgotten: 'I Love Little Pussy, Her Coat is So Warm'.

Guess which they started with.

That's right. The one I hate the most. 'I Love Little Pussy'.

Ellie was star of this show. The twins started bossing her about. 'Ellie, sit in front of the tree so all the sparkly decorations twinkle around you.'

'Be careful not to let Tuffy go. Remember what your dad said.'

'Tip your head to one side, and *smile*.'

'Spread out your skirts. You'll look like a princess!'

Oh, I don't think so! Ellie was dressed in that frilly-dilly party frock she grew out of years ago. If you want my

opinion, she looked more like an
overgrown cream puff than a princess.

The Two Big Dafties kept on
rearranging her. 'Put that arm more
closely round Tuffy.'

'And show your pretty ring. That's
right. Oh, Ellie! Now you look like
something out of a fairy tale!'

(She did too. Like a frog in a wedding
dress.)

They started in on *me*.

'Stop struggling, Tuffy. Try to look
happy for the show!'

I didn't see why I should try to look
happy. There I was, held too tight, and
stuck under that stupid tree. Pine
needles kept falling in my fur, and I was
worried that the great fat lump of a

Christmas fairy on the top would tumble through the branches on to my head. She's far too big and heavy for the tree. But Ellie made her, way back in nursery school, so everyone has to pretend she isn't the same shape as an exploding lavatory roll, and doesn't have a face that makes her look more like a squashed tomato than a pretty fairy.

6: Screams and tears

ALL RIGHT, ALL right! So spank me! I lost my temper. You would have lost yours too. (Faster than I did, probably.) I was so *sick* of being petted and fussed over and sung to by Ellie.

The trouble is that Ellie has a voice like one of those corncrake birds that are so famous for singing like two sticks being rubbed together. In fact, if you want my opinion, two sticks being rubbed together would make a much, much nicer noise than Ellie does when she sings.

Folding her arms round me, she began
that stupid song for the ninetieth time.

*'I love little pussy, her coat is so warm,
And if I don't hurt her she'll do me no harm.'*

Well, she was dead wrong, wasn't she?
Because it was a nasty scratch I gave her.
(Mind you, it was not *deliberate*. I was just
putting up a paw to try to stop her
stroking me. So how was I supposed to
guess that she had just decided her show
would be much better if she suddenly

leaned down to kiss me on the nose?

Me. A cat! Kissed on the nose! If you ask me, she was pretty well *asking* for trouble.)

As you can imagine, there were screams and tears. Her mum and dad and Uncle Brian and Aunt Ann rushed in to find out what was going on. And suddenly everyone was peering at this teensy-weensy little bead of blood on

Ellie's arm – you practically had to have a *microscope* even to see it – and Uncle Brian was running round and round in circles, shouting about rabies.

Rabies! I was a bit put out, I can tell you. For one thing, Ellie's had her shots. And, for another, it's mad dogs and bats and things that give you rabies, not a musically gifted cat who's simply had enough of hearing someone singing like two sticks rubbed together.

I tell you I was so fed up that I walked out. Nobody noticed because they were all still fussing over Ellie. And that's how I ended up inside a cupboard. All alone in the dark. Just two big staring eyes hiding from everyone, misunderstood as usual, and not at all looking forward to Christmas Day.

In fact, I was hoping that the whole idea of special little nursery rhyme shows would go away for*ever.*

7: Twanging the spider's web

BUT NO SUCH luck. All that they did was
stick a plaster on to Ellie's arm and move
on to a safer nursery rhyme.

'Ding Dong Bell, Pussy's in the Well'.

It wasn't a *real* well they planned to
put me in, of course. Lucilla and
Lancelot made it while Ellie was trying
to tempt me out of the cupboard with
some of Aunt Ann's quite delicious bite-
sized salmon tarts. (She is so posh she
calls them 'canapés'.)

The twins used the box the coffee
table came in. The two of them pulled
out the staples and flattened it. Then

they cut off the top, folded it into a circle and stapled it up again.

After they'd painted grey squares all over it, it looked like a stone well. They carried it into the living room. It seemed that Lancelot was to be the star of this part of the show. He found some red velvet knickerbocker trousers in the dressing-up box and pranced around singing, '*Who put him in?*' and '*Who took him out?*' over and over.

They didn't dare put me inside their stupid well.

'Wait till we've practised the song,' said Lancelot, giving me a worried look. 'It might be safer.'

'Yes,' Lucilla agreed. 'Let's not put Tuffy in there until we're sure that we've got everything right.'

Ellie looked down at the plaster on her arm, and then at me. 'Yes, Tuffy. You can be in the show *later*.'

I'd had enough of people telling me where I could or couldn't go in my own house. I gave a mighty squirm in Lucilla's arms.

Terrified, she let go.

I jumped straight in their silly well.

They were all thrilled. 'Oh, Tuffy! You're a genius!'

I raised my head and yowled.

They were all so excited. 'Look! Tuffy

can act! He can pretend that he's stuck down our well!'

'Oh, he's so *clever*!'

'Quick! Sing your song, Lancelot!'

So Lancelot started off again. '*Ding dong bell. Pussy's in the well. Who put her in?*' he warbled.

The girls sang, '*Little Tommy Lynn.*'

'*Who took her out?*' sang Lancelot.

'*Little Johnny Stout,*' sang Lucilla and the Corncrake.

'I get the next two lines!' said Lancelot, and started singing, '*What a naughty boy was that –*'

But the girls butted in, '*– to try to drown poor pussy cat.*'

Lancelot was getting cross. 'I am the star of this show! So I get to sing the last two lines all by myself.'

'No, you don't,' Lucilla argued. And she and Ellie sang together to try to drown him out:

'*Who never did him any harm,
But killed the mice in his father's barn.*'

I was so bored with listening to them singing and arguing that I settled down to watch a great fat hairy spider climb out of a staple hole inside the

cardboard well, and start on a new
web.

The spider was good fun to tease. I let
it spin a couple of lines, and then
reached out to twang one – not so hard
it broke, but just enough to set the
spider bouncing.

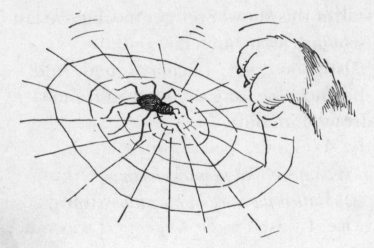

Spin, spin.
Twang, twang.
Bounce, bounce.

It was a laugh. I kept on doing it. But the spider was stubborn and kept on spinning. I was so busy twanging, I hardly noticed when The Three Bad Singers finished their stupid argument and started up again.

'*Ding dong bell!*' Lancelot sang loudly. '*Pussy's in the well!*'

'*Who put him in?*' chirruped Lucilla.

'*Little Tommy Lynn,*' gargled the Corncrake.

'*Who pulled him out?*' warbled Lucilla.

And that's when Lancelot reached over the side of the well to pull me out.

Well, don't blame me for everything that happened next! I already told you twice. I wasn't really *listening*. I was much more interested in twanging the web – a little harder each time. I don't see how I was supposed to know that suddenly I'd twang too hard, and the spider would lose its grip on the web and fly up in the air.

Or that it would be Lancelot's turn to sing the next line of the nursery rhyme.

So that his mouth would be open wide.

Very, *very* wide.

Okay, okay! So scream the house down, everyone! Lancelot swallowed a *spider*. What's the big deal? I've seen him eating fish. Fish are a whole lot bigger than spiders. (And they have creepy eyes.)

And he ate pork last night. That is a lump of dead pig's bottom. So why make such a fuss about an eensy-weensy spider? And anyway, it was already deep down inside him, getting mixed up with his lunch. So there was really no point in reeling round and round the room, screaming and gagging and spluttering.

That spider was inside to stay.

If anyone had any reason to make a
fuss, it was the poor old spider, not fussy
Lancelot.

Lucilla and Ellie were on my back, of
course. 'Tuffy, that was so *mean*!'

'That was a *horrible* thing to do, flicking
that spider into Lancelot's mouth!'

'Poor Lancelot!'

Poor Lancelot? I like that! Why should
Lancelot get all the sympathy? Who is it

who has spent the whole day locked in a room with the The Three Show-Offs?

Me, that's who.

So how about feeling sorry for *me*?

8: Chasing half-dead mousies

NOW IT WAS Lucilla's turn to be Star of the Show.

'Which nursery rhyme will you choose?' they asked her.

Lucilla hugged herself with glee. 'I'm going to sing *Pussy Cat, Pussy Cat, where have you been? I've been up to London to visit the Queen*. Then I can wear that lovely, lovely crown in the dressing-up box.'

(These three can get excited about *anything*. The jewels on that 'lovely, lovely crown' are stuck-on wine gums. I know that for sure because I've licked them.)

Ellie wasn't happy with Lucilla's choice. 'Oh, please don't let's do that one! I always cry when it gets to the bit that says, *Pussy cat, pussy cat, what did you there? I frightened a little mouse under her chair.*'

'Why?' Lancelot asked.

There was a silence. They all looked at me as if I was a criminal – as if I spent my *whole life* chasing half-dead mousies round the house.

I was offended, if you want to know. They wouldn't open the door, so I just went and sat under the Christmas tree, next to the presents.

Okay, okay. So I was *sulking*. But how is it *my* fault that my tail was flicking from side to side? I am a cat, and that's what happens to our tails when we get cross. My tail's a part of me. From my point of view, it's just the end of my bottom. You don't spend all day looking to see exactly what's going on at the end of your bottom, do you? Well, neither do I. So how was I supposed to notice that it was acting like a little furry brush, and flicking all those silly little labels off and out of sight, under the carpet?

It took them ages, but finally, *finally*, they managed to choose another rhyme for their show.

'"Three Little Kittens, They Lost Their Mittens",' decided Lucilla.

'Yes! Perfect!' Ellie said. 'We can use Tuffy and my two soft cat toys.'

'Use' Tuffy? Excuse me! What am I now? A kitchen towel, or something?

Nobody 'uses' me.

Now Lancelot was pitching in. 'And we'll need twelve little mittens.'

I looked up. Mittens? On *my* paws? Oh, no. No, no, no, no. Not even if they made me Star of the Show.

But they were already rushing off to look for what they needed. While they were gone, I had a laugh, reaching up to bat a few of the glittery balls off the tree. Just like last year, I gave myself five points if they fell down among the presents, and a bonus of five if they rolled on to the carpet.

I got a hundred and twenty points in all.

Excellent score! Even better than last year. But that's practising for you. You know what they always say: 'Practice makes perfect.'

9: Bare at the bottom

OKAY, OKAY! SO no one warned them
when they rushed back in. Three pairs
of feet can trample on an awful lot of
decorations before skidding to a halt.
So there were crispy bits of glittery ball
everywhere. All trodden in. Ellie's father
had to get out the vacuum cleaner, and
Ellie's mum spent ages picking tiny silver
slivers out of the fluffy slippers Aunt Ann
had left by the sofa.

Things were quite quiet after that,
apart from Ellie's father's constant
grumbling. 'I *knew* we should have kept
Tuffy behind bars. Look at that tree!

51

What a mess! Practically *bare* at the
bottom now. And overloaded at the top.
It looks quite shocking.'

You could tell
Ellie was worried I
might end up in the
cattery. She said, 'We
could move some of
the glittery balls that Tuffy couldn't
reach down to the lower branches.'

But Mr Didn't-Get-His-Way was in a giant snit. 'Why would you do that? Just to help the fiendish little beast smash all the ones he couldn't reach before?'

Did you hear that? I get accused of *everything*. *I* didn't smash the glittery balls. All that I did was set them rolling where they got trodden on. Is it my fault if people can't be bothered to look where they are putting their big fat feet?

I just gave him the cold cat stare as he went out. Then, sticking my paws over my ears, I tried not to listen as Ellie and Lancelot and Lucilla pranced about all afternoon, singing that great long boring nursery rhyme about the three prissy little kittens who spent their whole time losing their mittens, and finding their mittens, and getting their mittens dirty, and washing their mittens, and drying their mittens and –

Oh, excuse me. Their life's so dull I fell asleep just telling you about it.

Zzzzzzzzzzzzzzzzzzzz.

10: Chocolate coins and sausages

THAT NIGHT, IN Ellie's bedroom, The
Three Ninnies couldn't stop whispering
excitedly. 'Yippee! Christmas Day
tomorrow!'

'We'll wake to find our stockings on
our beds!'

'And we'll have sausages for breakfast!'

'Then we'll unwrap the presents under
the tree!'

'Eat a lovely big lunch!'

'And super-duper Christmas pudding!'

'Then everyone will come in the front
room to watch our show!'

'It'll be magic!'

I settled down on Ellie's bed. She put
her arms round me. 'Oh, Tuffy! I do
love you so.'

She's not so bad. I gave her a brief
purr. I was quite looking forward to the
stockings myself.

No such luck. Right in the middle of
the night a huge hand scooped me up
and dumped me out on the landing. 'I
think these stockings will be safer away
from you.'

Well, thank you, Santa! All the other doors were closed, so I just settled on a nice warm towel I pulled down from the bathroom rack. It wasn't a bad night, though I was woken ridiculously early by frantic squeals. 'Look! Santa's left our stockings!'

'Chocolate coins!'

'I've got a little jumping frog.'

'I've got a clockwork mouse.'

Oh, please! How *old* are Ellie and the twins? *Three*? You wouldn't catch me playing with a clockwork mouse – unless it was to push it into Aunt Ann's furry slippers and give her a heart attack.

But I still reckoned it would be more fun to watch them unpacking their stockings than to hang around the bathroom on my own.

So I jumped up on Ellie's bed.

She threw her arms round me. 'Oh,

Tuffy! Christmas is *magic*, isn't it? You think so too, don't you, even though you don't like chocolate coins.'

Who says I don't like chocolate coins? They're bright and gold and shiny, and fun to bat off the bed.

Okay, okay! So twist my tail! Some of the ones I batted went down that giant hole that Mr I-Can-Fix-It-All-By-Myself made in the floor when he was sorting out that leaking pipe. Is it my fault the hole's so deep she couldn't fish them out again?

No. It is *his*.

But not having quite so many chocolate coins as usual meant Ellie got hungry sooner. So we all went down for breakfast. There didn't seem to be too much Christmas Spirit coming my way. Nobody offered me a special breakfast. To get some sausages, I had to creep up beside Lancelot and jump in his lap, knocking his elbow.

Success! The sausage he was trying to cut flew off on to the floor.

If it had been a mouse, I couldn't have pounced faster.

Got it!

I reckoned it was safer to take my prize out in the garden. So I rushed through the cat flap.

The last thing that I heard behind me was Mr Not-Very-Nice bolting it closed behind me.

Well, happy Christmas to you too!

11: Showers of falling food

WHILE I WAS looking for a way back in, the grown-ups must have cleared away the breakfast things and started to prepare for Christmas lunch. By the time I had found the only bedroom window that was unlatched, and squeezed inside, the turkey was already stuffed and trussed, and sitting forlornly in its tray, waiting to go in the oven.

I ask you. Honestly! They all go on and on about the way that I chase sparrows. But I would *never* treat a bird like that.

Hypocrites!

Anyhow, once it was safely in the oven
(out of my reach) the four of them went
through to the front room, to join the
children, and unwrap the presents.

I had forgotten about the labels my tail
had accidentally flicked away, out of
sight under the carpet.

Uh-oh. The trouble started almost at
once.

'Who is this gift for? It doesn't say.'

'This one doesn't have a label.'

'Neither has this one. Or this.'

I couldn't help but look a bit uncomfortable. (I hadn't realized I'd flicked off so many.) The children rooted around, lifted their heads and wailed, 'We've looked at *all* the presents, and not one has a label.'

'What are we going to *do*?'

'We'll simply have to *guess*.'

That didn't work too well, and arguments broke out all over. 'I think this one is probably for me.'

'No, dear. I think that Santa brought that one for Lucilla.'

That set Lucilla off. 'But I don't want it, Mummy. I like this present much better.'

'But that one was meant for Ellie.'

'How do you *know*?'

'I just do, dear.'

'You can't read Santa's mind!'

'Neither can you!'

We were a little short on Christmas cheer. And then a scuffle started when Lancelot tried to snatch back a present that Ellie's father said was not for him. The carpet rucked up underneath his shoe, and there they were – all of the labels.

And one or two telltale ginger hairs,
off my tail.

'A-*ha*!' cried Ellie's father.

Everyone turned to look at me. I
turned to look at the door. I don't think
it was my fault that, just at the moment
that I fled towards it, Ellie's mother was
coming in carrying a giant plate of tiny
tarts and titbits and fancy little things on
sticks.

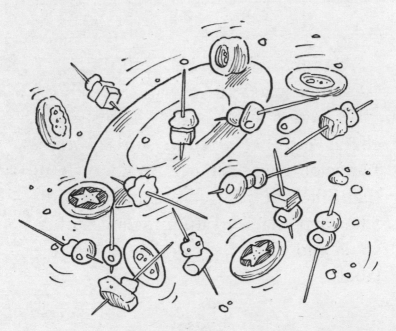

I just think I was lucky that, in the showers of falling food, I managed to get clean away.

12: Star of the show

I SKIPPED LUNCH. And the washing up. And all that fuss when Aunt Ann realized that there were lumps in her cake icing, and she would have to keep stirring.

I wasn't going back outside. Cold, wet and miserable. So I stayed out of sight, hiding in one of Uncle Brian's welly boots till I heard Ellie walk past.

'Tuffy! Tuff-eee!'

I stretched up in the boot to see which way she was headed. That was a big mistake. The boot began to wobble and I lost balance.

Out I spilled, on to the floor.

She scooped me up. 'Time for the show,' she told me. 'And guess who's going to be the star!' She nuzzled her nose in my fur. '*You* are! You're going to be the very best of all of us because you're so *clever*.'

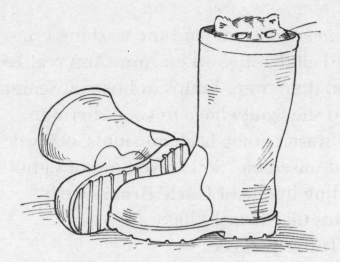

The best of them all! So *clever*! How can you run away and hide when someone as caring as Ellie thinks that you're the bees' knees? Call it the Christmas Spirit if you will, but suddenly

I felt mean, trying to sneak away after they'd worked so hard painting the well, and practising their songs, and making paper mittens for the two toy cats.

They'd even gone next door to borrow two tiny pairs of real woollen baby mittens they could fit on me.

How could I let them down?

So I gave up and let Ellie carry me into the front room. The cardboard well was on the rug. Lucilla and Lancelot were ready in their costumes. Aunt Ann had even stopped stirring her icing and put the mixing bowl safely down on the floor behind the sofa.

All of the grown-ups settled on the sofa, ready to watch. Even the huge fat fairy on the top of the Christmas tree seemed to be peering down and waiting for the show to start.

'Ready?' Lucilla asked.

Why not? I thought. Why not do
something nice for Ellie? Why not make
the best of things, and turn their stupid
little betsy-wetsy show into a *triumph*?

WOW them! Amaze them with my
wonderful acting skills! Help out The
Three Soft Noodles, and give the grown-
ups the surprise of their lives!

Tuffy, the Acting Cat. Star of the Show.

Everything started brilliantly. We did 'I
Love Little Pussy' first. When Ellie
tipped her head winsomely to one side, I
tipped mine even more winsomely to the
other. I stared so lovingly into her eyes. I
even purred. It was a shame the only
decorations left on the tree were all up
at the top, so they won't show up on the
photographs. But, still, Ellie and I made
a nice pair, and if it wasn't for her awful
corncrake voice, that bit of the show
would have been *perfect*. Certainly *I* was

excellent. I think I totally surprised her
dad. And Uncle Brian and Aunt Ann
and Ellie's mother clapped like mad
when the song ended.

Then it was 'Ding Dong Bell'.

That was a triumph too. I let them
put me in the well, then I crouched
down and hid, as if it was really deep.
I yowled a bit through the first verse,
making my voice sound tragic yet

musical. The scene was very moving.

Then we got to the bit where Lancelot pulled me out, and as I reached up to nuzzle him under his chin in pretend gratitude, I even saw Aunt Ann brush away a tear.

We all took a bow after that one. When the applause from the sofa finally died down, we moved on to the third and last show: 'Three Little Kittens'.

Lucilla set the two toy cats in place on the carpet. She and Ellie made sure their paper mittens were on straight. Then they pulled Next-door's baby's woollen mitts on to my paws.

I was such a star! I didn't even *struggle*. I actually held out each paw in turn to help. I could tell Ellie's father was pretty surprised to see me acting so sweet and easy-going. But he said nothing, just sat there, looking suspicious as usual.

And off we went. First I pranced around in my mittens to show I was wearing them. Then Ellie, Lancelot and Lucilla started on the first verse:

'*Three little kittens, they lost their mittens.*'

They tugged the paper off the toy cats' feet while I slipped behind the sofa to kick my own off by myself.

The trouble was, I kicked my mitten

booties off so hard, they slid under the sofa.

All the way under. Where I wouldn't be able to get at them later, when I needed them back.

No time to stop the show, so I came rushing back in time to rub my eyes with my paws as Lucilla and Lancelot and Ellie sang, '*And they began to cry.*'

Now it was Ellie's turn to act the Mother Cat, scolding us.

'What? Lost your mittens? You bad little kittens! Then you shall have no pie.'

Time to get back in my mittens. I scuttled round behind the sofa. But it was hopeless. Even if I stretched, I couldn't reach them.

So go on, all you big-heads out there, reading this. So what would *you* have done? Just given up?

Not me! I wasn't going to spoil the show. All that I needed was four white mittens. And there beside me was the bowl of icing for the cake.

Snow-white. Not too shallow. Not too deep.

And I was Star of the Show.

(Unlucky) 13: The fairy on the Christmas tree

OKAY, OKAY. SO I went paddling in the cake icing. Brilliant idea, I thought. When I walked into the show, I looked exactly as if I'd put the white woollen mittens back on perfectly, all by myself.

Nobody noticed at first. Ellie, Lucilla and Lancelot were busy singing.

'*Three little kittens, they* found *their mittens.*'

I pranced about. That was my big mistake, for Ellie's mother couldn't help noticing that I was leaving footprints – snow-white icing footprints – all over the carpet.

She pointed. 'Look!'

The singing stopped.

'Look at the mess Tuffy is making!' said Ellie's mother. 'What's that all over his paws?'

'It looks like –' Aunt Ann stood up and hurried round behind the sofa. We heard a shriek. It sounded like an express train screeching to a halt when a green light turns red.

Aunt Ann picked up the bowl and held

it out for all to see. 'Look! Look at my icing! It's ruined! All churned up, and full of paw marks!'

Ellie's dad went mad. 'That pest of a cat! This time he's gone too far! I warn you, the moment the vet's office opens up again after Christmas, I'm taking Tuffy down there to –'

'No!' Ellie hurled herself towards her father but, blinded by tears, she bumped into Lancelot. He knocked his sister, who fell in the well. I knew that, if Ellie's dad got hold of me, he'd have my guts for garters. So while Ellie's and Lancelot's legs and arms were madly flailing about, getting tangled, I tried to make it to the door.

But Mr I-Have-Had-Enough was blocking the way. So I rushed out of sight behind the sofa. Then, while Ellie pulled herself free and started to shout at her father – 'You leave poor Tuffy alone! You're *always* picking on him!' – I slid away, under the tree. There were no glittery balls to hide me in the bottom half, so I climbed up the back, branch by branch, higher and higher, while everyone was busy picking themselves up, and comforting Aunt Ann, and rushing off for cloths to clear up the icing footprints.

Now I was almost at the top. Only Ellie's fat cardboard fairy was higher.

And then I suddenly thought of a brilliant way to hide myself. I looked up at Ms Tomato-Face on top of the tree. 'This is the end for you, Sunshine!' I muttered to her. 'You have had your days of glory. Now move over. I am going to be the new Christmas fairy.'

I poked a paw up through her big fat cardboard roll. Her stupid red tomato face fell off and bounced a few branches down.

Creepy!

But I'd no time to hang about shivering. Hastily I shoved my head up through the space she'd left, and tried to put on the same snooty simpering look she'd worn for years.

Personally, looking back, I think the white frills probably suited me, and I looked *nice* in them. I rather wish they'd had the time to take a proper photo of their dear Tuffy as the new fairy at the top of the tree. I would have liked to show it to my friends.

But Ellie's dad was right. The tree was not just bare at the bottom; it was overloaded at the top.

Too overloaded.

What they call 'top heavy'.

It started toppling. It was far worse than being in the welly boot because I was much higher. It was like being in the crow's nest of some ancient galleon when it keels over in a storm.

It took a long time for the tree to fall. They were all fussing and yelling. 'Step back!'

'The tree is crashing down!'

'Watch out!'

'Look at this mess!'

'Our lovely well! Totally squashed!'

'There's not a single decoration left!
Smashed! Every last one of them!'
'I'm bruised all over.'
'Where is that damn cat?'

Well, I was on the floor, of course. Pretty
well splatted flat, still trying to be the
Christmas fairy. It was the ears that gave
me away. Christmas-tree fairies don't
have pointy little furry ears like mine.

So that explains how I ended up spending the rest of that day, and the next, locked in the garage. Ellie was only allowed to have me in her bedroom overnight, and then I was put back in here until the visitors go this afternoon and Christmas is over.

I don't mind. In fact, I think I've come out of this spat with her father quite well. After all, when you consider that Mr Let's-Take-Tuffy-Down-The-Vet's is stuck behind in the house, still picking bits of Christmas decoration out of the carpet, and doing all the washing up, I think I've got it easy. Popped hoppers are quite comfortable to laze around on. And now that moth's come back, I even have someone to play with. Certainly it's been a whole lot better than being in the house.

But, still, I won't be counting the days till 25th December comes round again. Remember that question you asked me at the start? 'Dear, dear Tuffy, *why* was your Christmas so horrible?'

Well, you won't have to ask again, will you?

Because now you know.

Roll Over Roly

"Jump, you
dozy lump!
Up! Down!
Faster!"

Rupert's puppy,
Roly, is so round and
warm and soft and lovely
that Rupert hasn't the
heart to be stern with him. It
looks as if Roly will *never* learn to behave.
But then he meets a parrot named Gordon...

'Can Anne Fine do no wrong?'
– *Books for Keeps*

'Anne Fine – infectiously funny and
highly readable' – *Independent*

Notso Hotso

So, suddenly one morning I'm like, *Scratch-scratch! Scratch-scratch!* and can't stop. It's disgusting.

It's a dog's life for Anthony. Not only is he lacking the respect he deserves from the neighbourhood dogs and cats, but bits of him are dropping off! And just when Anthony thinks things can't get worse, he finds himself on the vet's table. What she has in mind for him is likely to destroy the tiny shred of street cred he has left...

'...a fable about embarrassment that made me laugh aloud' – *Independent*

'A wickedly funny tale' – *Carousel*

It all started with a Scarecrow.

Puffin is seventy years old.
Sounds ancient, doesn't it? But Puffin has never been
so lively. We're always on the lookout for the next big
idea, which is how it began all those years ago.

Penguin Books was a big idea from the mind of
a man called Allen Lane, who in 1935 invented
the quality paperback and changed the world.
**And from great Penguins, great Puffins grew,
changing the face of children's books forever.**

The first four Puffin Picture Books were hatched in 1940 and the
first Puffin story book featured a man with broomstick arms called
Worzel Gummidge. In 1967 Kaye Webb, Puffin Editor, started the
Puffin Club, promising to **'make children into readers'**.
She kept that promise and over 200,000 children became
devoted Puffineers through their quarterly instalments of
Puffin Post, which is now back for a new generation.

Many years from now, we hope you'll look back and
remember Puffin with a smile. **No matter what your age
or what you're into, there's a Puffin for everyone.**
The possibilities are endless, but one thing is for sure:
whether it's a picture book or a paperback, a sticker book
or a hardback, **if it's got that little Puffin
on it – it's bound to be good.**